EXPLORING DINOSAURS & PREHISTORIC CREATURES

# COMPSOGNATHUS

*By Susan H. Gray*

THE CHILD'S WORLD®
CHANHASSEN, MINNESOTA

# The Child's World

Published in the United States of America by The Child's World®
PO Box 326, Chanhassen, MN 55317-0326
800-599-READ
www.childsworld.com

*Content Adviser:*
*Peter Makovicky,*
*PhD, Curator,*
*Field Museum,*
*Chicago, Illinois*

Photo Credits: Craig Lovell/Corbis: 15; Bettmann/Corbis: 22; Layne Kennedy/Corbis: 27; Linda Hall Library of Science, Engineering & Technology: 8, 18, 26; The Natural History Museum, London: 6, 7, 9, 13, 19; Roger Harris/Science Photo Library/Photo Researchers, Inc.: 4; Chris Butler/Science Photo Library/Photo Researchers, Inc.: 5, 20; Joe Tucciarone/Science Photo Library/Photo Researchers, Inc.: 10, 11; Joseph Nettis/ Photo Researchers, Inc.: 14, 17; Carlyn Iverson/Photo Researchers, Inc.: 21; Biophoto Associates/Photo Researchers, Inc.: 25.

The Child's World®: Mary Berendes, Publishing Director

Editorial Directions, Inc.: E. Russell Primm, Editorial Director; Katie Marsico, Associate Editor; Ruth Martin, Line Editor; Judith Shiffer, Assistant Editor; Matt Messbarger, Editorial Assistant; Susan Hindman, Copy Editor; Melissa McDaniel, Proofreader; Olivia Nellums, Fact Checkers; Tim Griffin/IndexServ, Indexer; Dawn Friedman, Photo Researcher; Linda S. Koutris, Photo Selector

Original cover art by Todd Marshall

The Design Lab: Kathleen Petelinsek, Design and Page Production

**Library of Congress Cataloging-in-Publication Data**
Gray, Susan Heinrichs.
 Compsognathus / by Susan H. Gray.
  v. cm. — (Exploring dinosaurs)
 Includes bibliographical references and index.
 Contents: An afternoon nap—What is a Compsognathus?—Who discovered
Compsognathus?—What were those other bones?—The world of Compsognathus—
Plenty to learn about Compsognathus?.
 ISBN 1-59296-233-5 (lib. bdg. : alk. paper) 1. Compsognathus—Juvenile literature.
[1. Compsognathus. 2. Dinosaurs.] I. Title.
 QE862.S3G6934 2005
 567.912—dc22                                    2003027073

# TABLE OF CONTENTS

# CHAPTER ONE

# AN AFTERNOON NAP

**C**ompsognathus (KOMP-sog-NATH-us) was stretched out, fast asleep. The warm sun shone down on the little dinosaur as she dozed. Dragonflies buzzed overhead. A lizard zipped by, leaving a trail in the dust.

*Compsognathus* was sleeping on her belly on a big rock slab. Her scaly underside soaked up the warmth of the rock. Her back took in the warm rays from above. As the sun moved across the sky, shade from some nearby trees

*In many ways,* Compsognathus *seemed more like a chicken than a ferocious reptile. It may have been related to a prehistoric creature called* Archaeopteryx *(AR-kee-OP-ter-ix). Some scientists believe* Archaeopteryx *was the first bird.*

*Compsognathus might have been small, but its size didn't stop it from being a highly skilled hunter. It was able to move quickly and had dangerously sharp teeth.*

crept over the sleeping **reptile.** Slowly, she opened one eye and then the other. She lifted her head and looked around. The sunny patch had moved far in front of her.

*Compsognathus* got up sleepily, took a few steps, then flopped back down in the sun. She scratched her neck, swallowed, and let out a sigh. In a few seconds, she was back in a deep sleep.

# CHAPTER TWO

# WHAT IS A *COMPSOGNATHUS*?

**C**ompsognathus was a dinosaur that lived about 150 million years ago. Its name is taken from Greek words that mean "pretty jaw" or "delicate jaw."

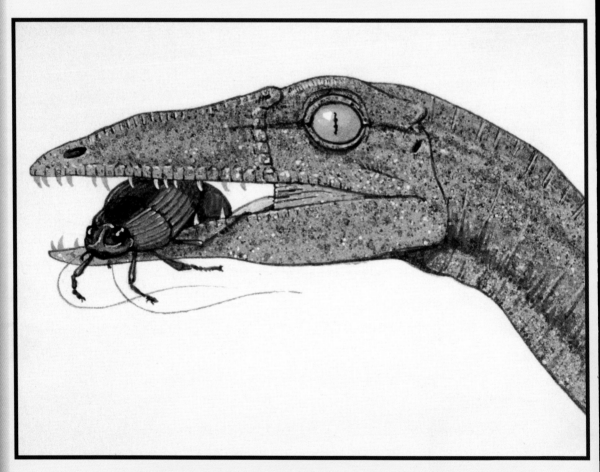

Compsognathus *used its delicate but powerful jaws to snap up insects, small lizards, and tiny mouselike creatures.*

*Most dinosaurs were bigger than* Compsognathus. *Although the large* Camarasaurus *(kam-AIR-uh-SAWR-uhss) shown in this picture were plant eaters, other prehistoric creatures probably hunted and ate* Compsognathus.

*Compsognathus* was one of the smallest dinosaurs that ever lived. Its body was only 18 to 24 inches (46 to 61 centimeters) long, and its tail was about the same length. The little dinosaur stood about 28 inches (71 cm) tall. It weighed a mere 6 to 8 pounds (2.7 to 3.6 kilograms). That's a little heavier than a chicken, but not as heavy as a house cat.

*Compsognathus*'s head was flat on top, and its eyes looked out to

*Compsognathus's little size and delicate bones enabled it to move swiftly. Larger dinosaurs such as* Allosaurus *(AL-oh-SAWR-uhss) and* Tyrannosaurus rex *(tie-RAN-uh-SAWR-uhss REX) would have clumsily crashed to the ground if they attempted to run as quickly as* Compsognathus.

opposite sides. Its mouth was filled with tiny, sharp teeth. The

reptile's neck was long and **flexible.** Its little arms were much

shorter than its legs. Each hand ended in two clawed fingers.

*Compsognathus* trotted around on its hind legs, holding its arms in

front or folded at its sides.

The legs of the dinosaur were long, thin, and built for running.

The upper part of the leg was strong and muscular, and the lower leg was slender. Each foot ended in three long toes pointing forward and one small toe pointing backward. Each toe ended in a sharp claw.

A long string of tailbones ran the length of the dinosaur's tail. This tells us that the dinosaur probably had a flexible tail that it used for balance. Such a tail may have prevented *Compsognathus* from toppling over as it made quick turns and sudden stops.

The little reptile had hollow bones with many spaces inside. Because of its light bones, slender body, and small size, *Compsognathus* was probably quite **agile.**

*To chase flying insects and speedy lizards, Compsognathus had to be both graceful and fast. Without its whiplike tail for balance, the dinosaur would have suffered quite a few falls and wouldn't have earned the reputation of being such a deadly hunter.*

## HOW DOES *COMPSOGNATHUS* STACK UP?

We know that dinosaurs came in all shapes and sizes. We also know they walked the earth for about 165 million years. So where does *Compsognath-us* fit in with the others?

Compared to the biggest dinosaurs, *Compsognathus* was a shrimp! One of the largest dinosaurs was the mighty *Supersaurus* (SOO-pur-SAWR-uhss). It was more than 100 feet (30 meters) long and weighed around 50 tons. That's more than 14,000 times the weight of *Compsognathus*!

*Compsognathus* lived

during the middle of the dinosaur age. The first dinosaurs appeared around 230 million years ago. *Compsognathus* did not show up until about 78 million years later. After the last *Compsognathus* died out, dinosaurs continued to roam the earth for another 80 million years.

The word *dinosaur* means "terrifying lizard." But was little *Compsognathus* really so terrifying? Well, lizards and other small prey surely ran from it. But compared to the big, meat-eating *Allosaurus* that lived at the same time, the chicken-sized *Compsognathus* was not terrifying at all.

# CHAPTER THREE

# WHO DISCOVERED COMPSOGNATHUS?

The first *Compsognathus* skeleton was found in southern Germany in the 1850s. **Quarry** workers discovered the skeleton within a limestone rock. It was in terrific shape. In fact, it is still among the most complete dinosaur skeletons ever discovered.

A German doctor named Johann Wagner bought and studied the skeleton. He compared it to other dinosaurs known at the time. It was Wagner who decided this was a new kind of dinosaur, one that had never been seen before. He gave it the official name *Compsognathus* in 1859.

For years, people marveled at the beautiful little skeleton. Its bones were fine and delicate. It was wonderfully preserved in stone. The dinosaur was locked in a position that scientists call the death

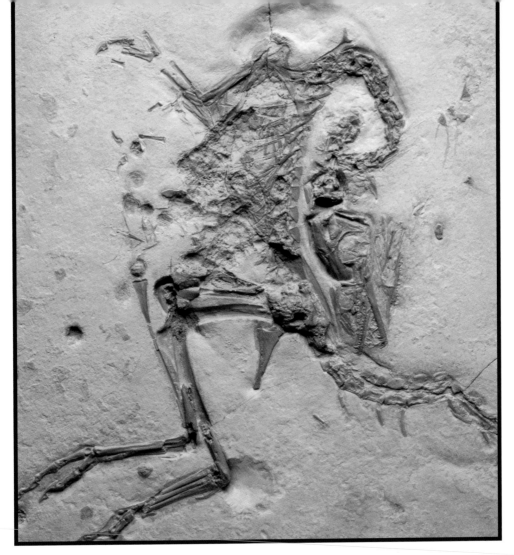

*This fossilized* Compsognathus *skeleton was discovered in southern Germany and is now located at the Natural History Museum in London, England.*

pose. Its neck was arched backward, and its head was near its back-

bone. This happened because after the dinosaur died, tissues in its

neck shrank and pulled the head back toward the spine. This was

such a nice **fossil** that scientists hoped to find more just like it.

*Large dinosaur fossils are easier for scientists to find than* Compsognathus*'s smaller and more fragile bones. Even with larger bones, however, scientists have to be extremely careful. In the 1800s and early 1900s, several prehistoric fossils were damaged beyond repair because they were handled too roughly.*

such a nice **fossil** that scientists hoped to find more just like it. Though many people searched, much time passed before another *Compsognathus* was found.

The dinosaur's small size and fragile bones are probably the reasons that finding a *Compsognathus* skeleton is so rare. Such small, delicate bones were not likely to last long when left lying on the ground. Other animals could easily eat them or the bones would quickly rot away. And if small bones were out in the wind or rain, they would probably blow or wash away. Also, fossil hunters might not see little bones, especially if they are looking for large dinosaur

Perhaps this explains why more than 100 years passed before the second *Compsognathus* was found. In the 1970s, quarry workers in France discovered this skeleton, which is larger than the German **specimen.** Like the skeleton in Germany, though, it was almost complete and was very well preserved. Today, these are the only two known *Compsognathus* skeletons.

*When searching for dinosaur remains, scientists and teams of workers often set up camp in quarries such as this one, which is located in France.*

# CHAPTER FOUR

# WHAT WERE THOSE OTHER BONES?

More than 20 years after the first *Compsognathus* was found, a famous paleontologist (PAY-lee-un-TAWL-uh-jist) took a closer look at it. Paleontologists are people who study the fossil remains of **ancient** life. They try to figure out how animals and plants lived long ago.

This paleontologist spotted a tiny skeleton within the *Compsognathus* rib cage. The skeleton was clearly from some kind of little reptile. But why was it in there?

The scientist decided that the bones could be one of two things. They might be from a baby *Compsognathus* about to be born. Or perhaps they were from a young *Compsognathus* that was eaten by an older one. Maybe, the scientist said, *Compsognathus* ate its own kind.

*Paleontologists are similar to detectives who are trying to solve mysteries of the past. By studying fossilized bones, footprints, and plant life, these scientists can often determine where and when a dinosaur lived, what it ate, and even how fast it moved!*

Twenty more years passed. Then another scientist said those

ideas just didn't sound right. So he, too, took a closer look at the

tiny skeleton. He decided that the little bones belonged to a lizard, not another *Compsognathus.* The lizard was probably the last meal

that the dinosaur ate.

Today, most paleontologists agree that the extra bones belonged

to a fast-running lizard. But the speedy *Compsognathus* was faster. It

snagged the little lizard and swallowed it quickly, leaving many of its

bones unbroken.

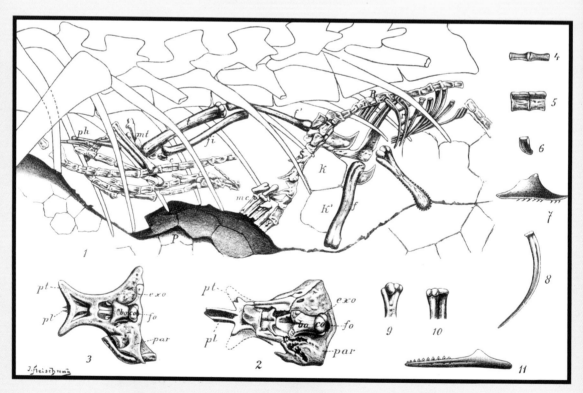

*This sketch shows the lizard skeleton that was discovered within the fossilized* Compsognathus *remains. Paleontologists also found evidence that the dinosaur was female and about to lay eggs.*

Compsognathus *(right)* probably did some of its hunting along prehistoric shorelines. In addition to eating lizards and insects, this quick little dinosaur might also have been a good fisher.

## IT IS GOOD TO BE LITTLE

When people think of dinosaurs, they usually think of big, ferocious, flesh-eating reptiles. Dinosaurs such as *Tyrannosaurus rex* often come to mind. People might also think of gigantic plant eaters. It might seem that bigger was better and that the bigger dinosaurs had a better chance of surviving. But was this really the case?

Big dinosaurs faced some problems that little ones did not. For one thing, the biggest dinosaurs needed several hundred pounds of food every day to survive. This meant they had to spend most of their time just finding food. A group of huge, plant-eating dinosaurs might strip a forest clean. When they got hungry again, they'd have to find another whole forest. A little *Compsognathus,* however, could probably get

by on a few lizards or small mammals a day.

In some cases, heavy dinosaur bodies might have been a problem. Some scientists wonder what would have happened if a large dinosaur tripped and fell as it ran. A dinosaur such as *T. rex* would probably break its tiny arms or other bones as its body crashed to the ground. But a dinosaur such as *Compsognathus* was already close to the ground. A stumble and fall for *Compsognathus* might have meant nothing more than a bloody nose.

Huge hunting dinosaurs had another problem. They sometimes had to sneak up on their dinosaur prey. But it's not easy to be sneaky when you're the size of a bus. If a sneaky predator was heard, it might have gotten bonked on the head with a tail club. *Compsognathus* didn't have that problem. Because it was a small, quick dinosaur, it could dart out, grab its prey, and finish it off. *Compsognathus* may have been little, but sometimes being little is a good thing.

# CHAPTER FIVE

# THE WORLD OF
# *COMPSOGNATHUS*

**C**ompsognathus lived during a time we call the Jurassic (jer-RASS-ik) period. The whole period lasted from 208 million to 144

*Dinosaurs such as* Stegosaurus *(STEG-oh-SAWR-uhss) and* Allosaurus *existed during the Jurassic period. Even after this period ended, dinosaurs continued to walk the earth for another 79 million years.*

million years ago. *Compsognathus* lived near the end of this period.

Plant and animal life was very different from that of the present time. As *Compsognathus* explored its **environment,** it may have run into cycads (SY-kadz). These plants looked like short palm trees and had tough, spiky leaves. Some cycads are still living today, but in the Jurassic period they were all over the place.

*Compsognathus* may also have seen a few ginkgo trees. These small trees with soft, fan-shaped leaves were quite common in the dinosaur's world. *Compsognathus's* environment was very dry, and some of the plants that lived there were able to store water in their stems.

When it grew hungry, *Compsognathus* would chase down one of the lizards, mammals, or insects in its area. The mammals it hunted were small and active, but probably not very fast compared to *Compsognathus.* One mammal might have been enough food for the whole day. A dragonfly or a cockroach might have been an evening snack.

If the little dinosaur gazed up at the sky, it probably saw reptiles soaring overhead. Some were no bigger than robins. Others were the size of small airplanes. Their heads were long and pointed, and their beaks were filled with teeth. With outspread wings, they floated on warm gusts of wind and searched for prey. A little *Compsognathus* might have ducked behind a rock as their shadows passed over.

If *Compsognathus* came to the seashore, it would have seen other animals. There, huge, sleek, swimming reptiles glided through the ocean waters. They used their fleshy paddles to thrust themselves forward, and their long tails snaked behind. Coming to the surface, the creatures sucked in air and then slipped below. *Compsognathus* certainly lived in a world different from the one we know today.

# CHAPTER SIX

# PLENTY TO LEARN ABOUT COMPSOGNATHUS

**D**espite having two excellent *Compsognathus* skeletons, we really know very little about the dinosaur. We do not even know

all the places where it lived. This is because we have so few fossils of

*Paleontologists don't simply study the fossil remains of ancient animals. Plant fossils such as the one shown here can tell scientists a lot about life in prehistoric times. These ginkgo leaves might provide clues about everything from climate to a dinosaur's diet.*

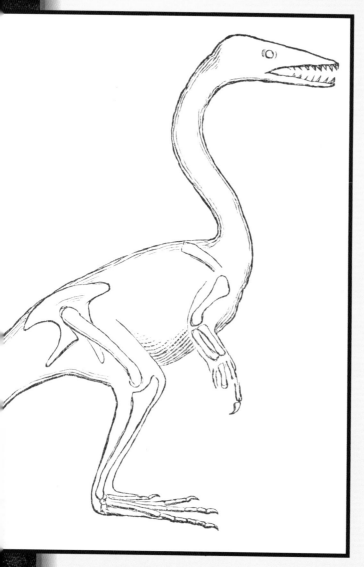

*Scientists still have several questions about the chickenlike* Compsognathus, *but at least they have two fossilized skeletons they are able to study. There could be hundreds of dinosaurs we don't even know about because they have yet to be discovered!*

the reptile. We know *Compsognathus* lived in Germany and France. But millions of years ago, the little reptiles might have run all over Europe.

Each time a new dinosaur fossil is found, it tells us more about the animal and how it lived. Suppose someone in Spain found a third *Compsognathus* skeleton. What would that tell us about where and how *Compsognathus* lived? Suppose that skeleton had tooth marks in it from another dinosaur. What could that tell us about the dinosaur's enemies? Suppose someone else found ten *Compsognathus* skeletons all together, and three of them were very small. What would paleontologists think about that?

Scientists today have many questions about *Compsognathus.* Perhaps someone will find another skeleton of the little reptile. Then we will have more clues about how this dinosaur lived.

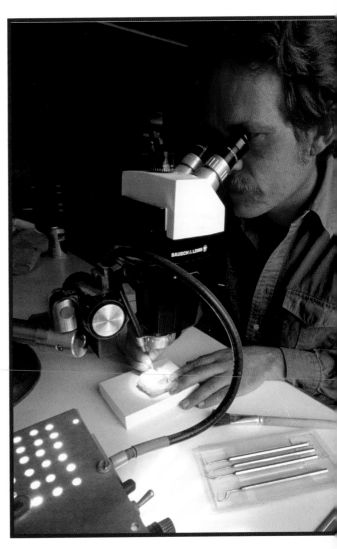

*Perhaps you'll grow up to be a paleontologist one day. It's exciting work but can also be quite frustrating and demanding. Many questions about prehistoric times require several years of digging in quarries or doing research before they can be answered.*

# Glossary

**agile (AJ-ile)** Something that is agile moves easily and at a quick pace. *Compsognathus* was among the more agile dinosaurs.

**ancient (AYN-shunt)** Something that is ancient is very old. Paleontologists study ancient life.

**environment (en-VYE-ruhn-muhnt)** An environment is made up of the things that surround a living creature, such as the air and soil. Cycads probably existed in *Compsognathus*'s environment.

**flexible (FLEK-suh-buhl)** Something that is flexible bends easily. *Compsognathus*'s neck was flexible.

**fossil (FOSS-uhl)** A fossil is something left behind by an ancient plant or animal. Two excellent *Compsognathus* fossils have been found, but scientists still have many questions about the dinosaur.

**prey (PRAY)** Prey are animals that are hunted and eaten by other animals. *Compsognathus* hunted lizards and other small prey.

**quarry (KWOR-ee)** A quarry is where workers dig stone from the ground. The first *Compsognathus* skeleton was found in a German quarry.

**reptile (REP-tile)** A reptile is an animal that breathes air, has a backbone, and is usually covered with scales or plates. *Compsognathus* was a reptile.

**specimen (SPESS-uh-muhn)** A specimen is a sample that is used to represent an entire group. The first *Compsognathus* specimen was discovered in the 1850s.

# Did You Know?

▸ *Compsognathus* belongs to a group of dinosaurs called theropods (THER-uh-podz). These were hollow-boned meat eaters that included *Tyrannosaurus rex*.

▸ Because *Compsognathus* seemed so birdlike, artists sometimes show it with feathers. However, some paleontologists believe that this is incorrect. Fossil remains of *Compsognathus* show no feathers at all. This might be because small feathers usually don't preserve well.

▸ Some scientists believe that *Compsognathus* may have had three-fingered hands, rather than two-fingered hands. The third finger is thought to have been shorter than the other fingers.

# How to Learn More

## AT THE LIBRARY

Lambert, David, Darren Naish, and Liz Wyse.
*Dinosaur Encyclopedia.* New York: DK Publishing, 2001.

## ON THE WEB

Visit our home page for lots of links about *Compsognathus*:
*http://www.childsworld.com/links.html*
NOTE TO PARENTS, TEACHERS, AND LIBRARIANS: We routinely verify our Web links
to make sure they're safe, active sites—so encourage your readers to check them out!

## PLACES TO VISIT OR CONTACT

AMERICAN MUSEUM OF NATURAL HISTORY
*To view numerous dinosaur fossils, as well as*
*the fossils of several ancient mammals*
Central Park West at 79th Street
New York, NY 10024-5192
212/769-5100

CARNEGIE MUSEUM OF NATURAL HISTORY
*To view a variety of dinosaur skeletons, as well*
*as fossils related to other extinct animals*
4400 Forbes Avenue
Pittsburgh, PA 15213
412/622-3131

DINOSAUR NATIONAL MONUMENT
*To view a huge deposit of*
*dinosaur bones in a natural setting*
Dinosaur, CO 81610-9724
              *or*
DINOSAUR NATIONAL MONUMENT (QUARRY)
11625 East 1500 South
Jensen, UT 84035
435/781-7700

MUSEUM OF THE ROCKIES
*To see real dinosaur fossils, as well as robotic replicas*
Montana State University
600 West Kagy Boulevard
Bozeman, MT 59717-2730
406/994-2251 or 406/994-DINO (3466)

NATIONAL MUSEUM OF NATURAL HISTORY
(SMITHSONIAN INSTITUTION)
*To see several dinosaur exhibits and special*
*behind-the-scenes tours*
10th Street and Constitution Avenue NW
Washington, DC 20560-0166
202/357-2700

# The Geologic Time Scale

## CAMBRIAN PERIOD

**Date:** 540 million to 505 million years ago
Most major animal groups appeared by the end of this period. Trilobites were common and algae became more diversified.

## ORDOVICIAN PERIOD

**Date:** 505 million to 440 million years ago
Marine life became more diversified. Crinoids and blastoids appeared, as did corals and primitive fish. The first land plants appeared. The climate changed greatly during this period—it began as warm and moist, but temperatures ultimately dropped. Huge glaciers formed, causing sea levels to fall.

## SILURIAN PERIOD

**Date:** 440 million to 410 million years ago
Glaciers melted, sea levels rose, and the earth's climate became more stable. Fish with jaws first appeared, as did the first freshwater fish. Plants with vascular systems developed. This means they had parts that helped them to conduct food and water.

## DEVONIAN PERIOD

**Date:** 410 million to 360 million years ago
Fish became more diverse, as did land plants. The first trees and forests appeared at this time, and the earliest seed-bearing plants began to grow. The first land-living vertebrates and insects appeared. Fossils also reveal evidence of the first ammonites and amphibians. The climate was warm and mild.

## CARBONIFEROUS PERIOD

**Date:** 360 million to 286 million years ago
The climate was warm and humid, but cooled toward the end of the period. Coal swamps dotted the landscape, as did a multitude of ferns. The earliest reptiles walked the earth. Pelycosaurs such as *Edaphosaurus* evolved toward the end of the Carboniferous period.

## PERMIAN PERIOD

**Date:** 286 million to 248 million years ago
Algae, sponges and corals were common on the ocean floor. Amphibians and reptiles were also prevalent at this time, as were seed-bearing plants and conifers. However, this period ended with the largest mass extinction on earth. This may have been caused by volcanic activity or the formation of glaciers and the lowering of sea levels.

## TRIASSIC PERIOD

**Date:** 248 million to 208 million years ago
The climate during this period was warm and dry. The first true mammals appeared, as did frogs, salamanders, and lizards. Evergreen trees made up much of the plant life. The first dinosaurs, including *Coelophysis*, walked the earth. In the skies, pterosaurs became the earliest winged reptiles to take flight. In the seas, ichthyosaurs and plesiosaurs made their appearance.

## JURASSIC PERIOD

**Date:** 208 million to 144 million years ago

The climate of the Jurassic period was warm and moist. The first birds appeared at this time, and plant life was more diverse and widespread. Although dinosaurs didn't even exist in the beginning of the Triassic period, they ruled the earth by Jurassic times. *Allosaurus, Apatosaurus, Archaeopteryx, Brachiosaurus, Compsognathus, Diplodocus, Ichthyosaurus, Plesiosaurus,* and *Stegosaurus* were just a few of the prehistoric creatures that lived during this period.

## CRETACEOUS PERIOD

**Date:** 144 million to 65 million years ago

The climate of the Cretaceous period was fairly mild. Many modern plants developed, including those with flowers. With flowering plants came a greater diversity of insect life. Birds further developed into two types: flying and flightless. Prehistoric creatures such as *Ankylosaurus, Edmontosaurus, Iguanodon, Maiasaura, Oviraptor, Psittacosaurus, Spinosaurus, Triceratops, Troodon, Tyrannosaurus rex,* and *Velociraptor* all existed during this period. At the end of the Cretaceous period came a great mass extinction that wiped out the dinosaurs, along with many other groups of animals.

## TERTIARY PERIOD

**Date:** 65 million to 1.8 million years ago

Mammals were extremely diversified at this time, and modern-day creatures such as horses, dogs, cats, bears, and whales developed.

## QUATERNARY PERIOD

**Date:** 1.8 million years ago to today

Temperatures continued to drop during this period. Several periods of glacial development led to what is known today as the Ice Age. Prehistoric creatures such as glyptodonts, mammoths, mastodons, *Megatherium*, and sabre-toothed cats roamed the earth. A mass extinction of these animals occurred approximately 10,000 years ago. The first human beings evolved during the Quaternary period.

# Index

## About the Author

**Susan H. Gray** has bachelor's and master's degrees in zoology and has taught college-level courses in biology. She first fell in love with fossil hunting while studying paleontology in college. In her 25 years as an author, she has written many articles for scientists and researchers, and many science books for children. Susan enjoys gardening, traveling, and playing the piano. She and her husband, Michael, live in Cabot, Arkansas.